To Pat and Tom
~ Britta

CATERPILLAR BOOKS
An imprint of the Little Tiger Group
www.littletiger.co.uk
1 Coda Studios, 189 Munster Road, London SW6 6AW
First published in Great Britain in 2019
Text and illustrations copyright © Britta Teckentrup 2019
A CIP Catalogue record for this book
is available from the British Library
All rights reserved • Printed in China
ISBN: 978-1-84857-877-7 • CPB/1800/1477/0520
10 9 8 7 6 5 4 3

Britta Teckentrup

Kindness
Grows

LiTTLE TiGER
LONDON

It all
    starts
        with a
            crack
        that we can hardly see,

It happens when we shout

or if we disagree.

But
with
every
kindness
that we care to show

Something good and magical

will begin to grow.

Friendships can be damaged
by a mean
or ugly word,

Once it has been spoken,
it cannot be unheard.

Words of encouragement,
sweetness,
warmth
and care

Blossom, grow and flourish
as they spread love everywhere.

If we leave friends abandoned,
   sad and on their own,

      Soon the crack will widen

and we'll be left alone.

Sharing things with others,
making a new friend,

May begin a journey

we hope will never end.

It's so hard to be friendly
when all we feel is sad.

Sometimes we are thoughtless,
and make other folk feel bad.

But a kindly thought or action
can make somebody's day.

If we keep our friends close by,
we won't drive them all away.

When we argue with each other

or we refuse to share,

The crack grows ever wider,
but we don't know it's there.

Playing all together

is always much more fun.

We have lots of space here
for each and everyone!

Sometimes we are selfish,

we shout and stamp our feet,

Feeling cross and angry
with everyone we meet.

But when we work together,

just look what we can do!

Anything is possible,
when one plus one makes two.

Anger can consume us until we just can't see

The beauty that's around us –
the moon, the stars,
a tree...

If we lean on one another,

and keep our friends around,
We make each other happy,
warm and safe and sound.

The crack has grown so wide now –
can we put things right?

If we reach out to others,
then maybe we just might...

It only takes a gesture –
a smile can be the start,

seed of friendship
omebody's heart.

Reaching out to others
is not as tricky as it seems...

... If we all join together,
we can chase our dreams.

Our tree will
grow much stronger,

the more we show
we care,

Built from
love and kindness

and the friendships
that we share.